THE GIANT LUMBERMEN OF STILLWATER

DANIEL REHM

THE GIANT LUMBERMEN OF STILLWATER

Daniel Rehm

The characters and events portrayed in this book are fictitious. Any similarity to real persons, living or dead, is coincidental and not intended by the author.

Paperback ISBN-13: 979-8-9928213-0-7
Digital e-book ISBN-13: 979-8-9928213-1-4

Cover design by: Rudbeckia Productions
Cover images provided by: Sandra, IG Digital Arts, Michael Rosskothen, tsuneomp, and Rawpixel.com

Rudbeckia Productions, LLC
North Branch, MN 55056
www.RudbeckiaProductions.com
www.DanRehm.com

Dedicated to the mighty Bome,
the last of his kind.

Chapter One

The Doorsteps of Giants

Goliath, a name, a proper noun that over time morphed into an adjective, bequeathing itself to all things large. Let it not be forgotten that Goliath was a biblical giant, *the* biblical giant. A Philistine who challenged the Israelites to put forth their greatest warrior, the winner to own dominion over the opposing army as slaves.

David saw the whole thing differently, his own king told him he had no shot, pun intended. David even refused the king's armor after trying it on. He told Saul he wasn't used to it. For those who don't know, David won. No sword, no shield, just a small bag of round stones and a sling. He buried one in Goliath's forehead and then used his enemy's own sword to cut off his head.

The point is a question, and the answer is yes, there were most definitely giants. Goliath is a prime example. Not only does he appear in what millions of people consider to be an official text, his description seemed accurate. Six cubits and a span which is close to nine feet six inches tall. A height that compliments archeological finds sequestered by those who perpetuate the status quo.

Jack and his farcical beanstalk have all but ruined gianthood forever. Ever since fee, fi, fo fum, children have been convinced giants were huge, lumbering, man eating beasts barely wise enough to string together a sentence that may or may not rhyme with a series of made up words.

In reality, giants have appeared in folklore across the globe and North America is no different. Native tribes from coast to coast and top to bottom have described giant "men". Some were said to have had multiple rows of teeth and fed on humans. Others were described as having red hair and wore armor as they went to war with the tribes. Mountainous giants had black faces and wore bear fur, appearing as ape-like animals. All were large, powerful, and apprehensive to be seen.

Mound building ancients, prolific in the midwest of the continental united states laid giants to rest in mass graves in Wisconsin, Minnesota, Ohio, and Michigan. It is unknown whether they buried their own, or they were inhumed by those who would have killed them. The latter seems plausible as the problem for giants has always been a numbers game.

As previously mentioned, this information is largely sequestered, erased from history by those from the likes of the Smithsonian and others of their ilk who confiscated the remains and dismissed the suddenly nonexistent findings as folklore and rumor.

Maybe someday the record will be set straight. In the meantime, it's up to those who know the old stories, the inadvertent keepers of true history, to share what they know, what they've heard, what they've seen.

One such person does exist, at least for now, tucked away on the top of a Dutchtown roadside turret, a stone's throw from the Saint Croix River in downtown Stillwater, Minnesota. He demanded anonymity, his name and likeness never to be known lest his descendants be left to incur the wrath of the bully pulpit.

He asked to be referred to as The Old Man, for his was a story of old men, his father as well as his grandfather, one of the original inhabitants of the town. And giants, old men and giants as they were also quite aged. Most lived twice the years of the oldest men, occasionally by a factor of three or more.

The Old Man was not sure of his own age although a century wouldn't have been a stretch. Unlike his father he was born and raised in Stillwater, but he could not recall anyone else speaking of them, the giants. When he was the youngest of boys he himself candidly recalled meeting one of them, maybe the last of them, and their ensuing relationship.

"His name was Kwah, like stick out your tongue and say ahh, except with a hard K and a 'W' at the beginning. Most of their words started with a 'K' sound, or a 'C' sound. Depends on how you'd spell it. Too many teeth for a bunch of other stuff. Guys who spoke English, which believe me wasn't all that many, thought they were stupid because of how they talked. Super deep voices too, like big drums. Well it figures, their chests were like this." The Old Man held his arms out forming a circle in front of him as far as he could reach.

"Trust me, they weren't dumb, just not much for conversation. They'd speak native though, probably better than English but we'd never know. I've heard tale of them giants knowing German and even conversing with Swedes as hard as those people are to hear," The Old Man said.

The Old Man's version of giant history is as unverifiable as it was frightening. Where they came from, how they came to be here, how they used to be versus how they eventually came to survive in the presence of so many new humans. He even knew what happened to them and if there are still any around.

Most importantly The Old Man knew what happened in Stillwater, way back when, just before it officially became Stillwater. He knew what the giants did to the poor, unsuspecting, ill-prepared settlers who thought it was a good idea to build here, on the doorsteps of giants.

"My father was a big man, Fin, a woodsman. Cold meant nothing to him. His hands, his hands were covered in thick, rough skin. He could scratch my scalp just rubbing the top of my head. And compared to his father, my grandfather didn't even barely consider him a man. Papa used to joke that his father was made of wood and stone. Another man would have to drill a hole in him just to make him bleed. Compared to the giants though, he was like a child."

"They were big across the shoulders, even wider than what would be normal for a huge man. As wide as a man could reach." The Old Man held his arms outstretched side to side as far as he could muster.

He told tales of giants hauling saw cut logs out of the woods and laying them onto wagons.

"They didn't use horses to drag 'em out, didn't need 'em. They just picked 'em up and laid 'em across their shoulders like a yoke, turned sideways to make it through when it was too thick. Most of them mill logs, wide white pine at least two feet across, sometimes closer to four and every inch of twenty feet end to end."

"They just leaned their heads forward don't ya know. The back of their necks were so wide, like a fat market hog. Didn't even need to use their hands to hold 'em steady. Heads were more like mounds of meat and muscle, big lumps, domes with thick hair. Hair like fur. When I was about this high Kwah said he took a black powder round just above the ear and dug it out with the jawbone of the man who put it there after he rushed up on him and punched his head apart. That's how I knew it was black powder cause the man was too busy reloading to have the good sense to run for his life."

The Old Man laughed, he knew Kwah well.

"That was one of the first stories he done told me. Tryin' to impress me I guess. I was scared stiff to listen to every word he said. You couldn't help it, his voice just rattled through ya', shook your innards. Like I said I was this high," he held out his hand in front of him about three feet off the ground.

"And hell, I barely come up to his kneecap. I could have slid down the hill on his foot, longer and wider than the old toboggan we pulled our gear on. Up and down, it's all rocks and hills up there by the river. Most men didn't go up that far, scared of course. A hell of a lot of 'em that did never came back."

"I guess they made their own shoes, their own clothes too. There was women folk after all, children, just not many. I was always of the understanding that was one the problems with giants. The oldest ones were old, damn old. You ever notice the bark on a really old tree? Thick, rough, and them giants was no different. Thems that was younger saw what a human woman looked like and compared to them tree looking females they were livin' with, well, let's just say they became attracted. And all told, the giant race weren't all that fertile to begin with. She wasn't always ready like a human woman, had a window of time when she was in heat. Even if that went according to plan she'd carry the child for more than two years. Now a female anything anywhere that's carrying for two years has got to be the most feared beast the almighty ever put down on this here Earth."

"Funny part is the giant females still wanted their big men. A human man, even the largest would be spindly and weak, probably wouldn't even survive the experience. I've heard some stories, not for the faint of heart. She's likely to pull some parts of a man clean off."

"Consequently, the giant women hated the hell out of settler girls, native girls too but at least they were smart enough to stay away. Or be kept away. The white women, well, the big giant girls could cook. A body don't get that big without having one hell of a lot of food. Settlers were taking up all the deer and moose, woodland caribou was all but gone."

"Giants on the other hand been here since the ice wore off. Everything was big back then, meat was plentiful. When the biggest animals started to go away the only thing left was people. That's how come they came to be known as man eaters. And like I said, the big girls could cook. Giant men, after they started to take down the forest were just too busy too hunt. At the end of the day they didn't care where the food came from, as long as it was hot and on the bone. Lots of girls in pretty bonnets never came out of the woods. Settlers blamed the natives as the big girls just smiled ear to ear every time one of their giant men would take a bite."

"Every one of them was like a king, dominant over all he come across, buffalo, bear, or man. Include in that the mammoths and mastodons that had already been gone. But they were spread thin across the country. A human can have three babies before they could have one. Numbers for all the reasons I already said were never their strong suit. And like I also said they weren't dumb neither."

"They finally figured the only way they were going to go along was going to be to get along. They saw what the white men were doing, cutting down all them trees and they knew they could do it better and a damn site faster. So they came together, being as how there is strength in numbers and struck a deal. We'll send you all the wood you want and in return you send us meat. We'll leave you alone, and you will do the same for us."

"The more forests they cut, the more room people had to raise beef, the more houses could be built. Problem was trees are a lot like giants. They don't reproduce all too fast, at least not to a serviceable size. After a while, the giants got concentrated to the river valley, to the white pines up north which were quickly running out. But none of that amounted to any sort of matter anyways, fate and circumstance seen to that, and Horace. Ruined every damn day you had to see him."

Chapter Two

The Gathering

Some of the furthest away from the area north of Stillwater were among the first to arrive. The native peoples of the southwest called them Si-Te-Cah, red-haired giants whom the Paiutes believed arrived from the sea. They have also come to be known as the Lovelock Giants, named for the cave where they made their final stand against the Paiutes. They were thought to have been wiped out but a handful managed to escape.

Kwah was among those who fled from Lovelock, a dried up former lake basin in western Nevada. As far as where the giants originally came from, his level of certainty was dubious at best.

Based on oral historical descriptions of landscape and weather, western Europe was their likely former home. Men were becoming too plentiful, and although some chose to stay and war with the smaller, easy to defeat humans, theirs was a life of quiet solitude. At least at first. It wasn't until food became scarce in the Americas that they began to eat the natives, humans they deemed to be inferior in every way.

The connotation that they were cannibals was by its own definition completely false. They were not people eating people, they were giants, and they did not feed on their own species. People were quite simply game.

Humans were by comparison slow and weak. As far as the giants were concerned the human's crude weapons were akin to a duck bite, and they fancied themselves entertained watching the people try so hard to fight back. A human's only respite was to climb a tall tree that was too meaty at the trunk to be torn from the ground, but also too thin for a giant to climb. Smaller holes and caves also functioned as sufficient hiding places but sore losers able to relocate 1,000 lb. stones were known to entomb their prey and return when they suspected the harvest to be somewhat easier.

As far as table fare, humans were soft with relatively thin skin. They didn't have much hair and they cooked quickly.

The hearts were said to be an especially delicious delicacy. Male giants would mock each other with severed human penises, sneaking them into each other's food and drink for a hearty laugh at the recipient's expense.

"They would fight over hearts," Kwah said.

A keystone moment in the red-haired giant's timeline occurred when the first boats appeared on their home shores. Likely Phoenicians, or possibly Minoans, the earliest ancient maritime explorers would have had some experience with their own giants and bid a hasty retreat upon first contact. This would explain the lack of archaeological evidence of their arrival. According to giant folklore, the incursion by water was met with swift and terrible offense, resulting in a quick death for the explorers.

The reason they killed first and asked questions later was because the new people came from the sea. Giants feared water especially the ocean and, by association, everything either in it or on it. The water was undrinkable and the tiniest creature may level them incapacitated or dead in a very short amount of time from a sting or bite they could barely feel.

Giants were by nature and body composition, unable to swim. They would ford hard-bottom rivers and streams out of necessity, but deep water left them no chance at survival. Even mires and shallow ponds were hazards. Due to their extreme weight, giants sank disproportionately deep, often becoming trapped, occasionally leading to death.

All of the boats were destroyed besides one. A small contingent of youth were enamored by the floating vessels. They longed to conquer that which gave them fear reasoning if the little men could do it, so could they.

The story goes that three of them, two of them brothers, set the boat out to sea. The third among them, Koros was the youngest and unrelated. He was also known as possibly the largest male giant to ever exist in the clan. It was said that he could crush a man's skull with just his thumb and forefinger. Without the basic knowledge of a rudder or setting sails, The Three as they would come to be known were at the mercy of the currents and waves, which quickly took them out to deep water.

As the rest of the party dispatched to destroy the boats watched from the safety of the sand, the procured boat turned parallel to the shoreline and moved away at a significant speed, eventually disappearing out of sight. The three aboard were given up for dead, and the giant's collective fear of the sea strengthened.

Upon the wane of the fourth moon post departure, a boat was once again spotted off shore, sails aloft, crashing the surf towards the shoreline where the burned hulls of the other ships still remained. The giants quickly amassed on the sand, ready to repel the newest invaders. Much to their shock, The Three had returned, wiser to the ways of sea, baptized by storm and distance as competent sailors. As the boat skidded to the sand still some distance from shore, the Koros jumped overboard much to the gasps of the former repellent force.

In chest deep water he grasped a rope tied to the bow and dragged the vessel the rest of the way to shore. The two brothers, after furling and stowing the sails also disembarked and helped him beach the ship. The elders commanded that The Three be destroyed but those who would do the bidding were hesitant to slay their own.

Prior to the potentially ensuing clash, The Three begged a chance to explain themselves, to plead with the clan.

Yes the sea was dangerous but it could be conquered. They explained that the sea was bountiful and they need not be afraid.

The Three shared with the clan the spoils of their journey. Fruits harvested from the south, fruits that would not be ripe where they lived until at least the next moon. Cisterns of fresh water in containers left on board by the original sailors, replenished by The Three. They told tales of endless coastal rivers, brimming with fish, flowing into the sea. And finally, meat and skins of the Vibrant Ox, a species few have seen as traveling south to the great plains where they roamed was fraught with peril. Hunting for them had been previously banned by the elders as almost all who attempted the journey overland did not return.

Koros proclaimed plans to build a bigger boat. Large enough for many giants and oxen. As the Vibrant Oxen were the only animals known to them that could match the giants in size and strength. As mighty beasts of burden they could be used to build, to war, and to feed the clan forever. His plan was to harvest the Ox, to take them alive as they were plentiful and nearly tame.

The civil war in the clan cut their numbers by half. In the end, Koros and the younger giants seized control. Two great ships were built, their size unrivaled among ancient sea-going vessels. They were in essence giant cargo ships and served as designed until fear changed the game.

Men of the time spotted the giant ships on the sea and were afraid. With much smaller and lighter boats they were able to hide and flee, often undetected by the less experienced giant crews. Humans had a number of advantages but most important were numbers and experience with war.

Koros and his crew were killed in the attack as their great ship was repeatedly rammed and burned until it finally broke apart. During the battle, the humans dared not board the giant's boat but many were killed as the giants jumped from ship to ship, cutting them down with oversized clubs, axes, and swords. For the giants, there was just too many to fight. The second ship, trailing some distance behind, dashed onto a reef that the smaller and faster human vessels could easily pass over. Those onboard could only watch, helplessly unable to swim to aid their brethren.

After the battle, the ship on the reef was saved and was able to return home. After repairs it was used as a lifeboat to take the remaining giants to the new lands where the numbers of men may never find them.

The Red Hairs were not alone. The influx of man was occurring across the globe, giants were being dispersed and their ancient cultures erased from history.

By the end of American Colonialism, giants in the eastern mountains had been nearly wiped out. Not by war or famine but by dispersion. An individual giant can survive but cannot thrive without a community of its own kind. For a tribe of giants in the Americas, there were few places left to hide.

American giants were mostly Mountain Giants, either Appalachian or Rocky. They were not as large as the Red Hairs and were decidedly less developed socially. They ranged deep into the Canadian Rockies as well and enjoyed the lush forests of the northwest. They did not wear clothing and had heavily haired bodies. Their vocalizations were also less astute, but none the less effective amongst themselves. They were athletic and elusive, using their environments to seemingly disappear at will.

Although appearing nearly apelike, they were highly intelligent and mostly peaceful. Some native tribes of humans worshipped them as Gods. They were one with nature, symbiotic to the environment, and left little to no trace. The opposite of men.

Very few of these American Giants joined the Red Hairs, most just happened to already be living in the area.

The rest of the clan north of Stillwater was a conglomerate of giant mutts from around the world. Some wore loin cloths and had only one eye right in the middle of their faces, the venerable cyclops from the lush Mediterranean. Mighty but not very bright.

Middle eastern giants wore turbans woven from enough cloth to completely cover a man. With long, flowing robes and huge, curved swords they were among the most intimidating of all giants. Complementing their sun-browned skin were colorless eyes that appeared to look through the men whom with they served. War was the culprit of their demise and the last of any known survivors traveled a great distance to be with those at Stillwater.

Giants of the African continent had been extinct for eons, their legacies lost to unwritten history, likely wiped out by hordes of men.

South America was a different story. Lush jungle habitat coupled with a sparse population meant the giants of the continent had no reason to flee. The great and powerful native societies revered them, even prayed to them. They were said to be quite a bit smaller than their northern cousins but still noticeably larger than the largest man. They have been depicted as more man-like, less hair covered and also one with their natural surroundings.

The giants of the far east also had no reason to fell. They lived well with humans, sharing cultures and customs until they were assimilated into the vast population.

Last but not least, among the giants was the last of his unknown species. He had no name that Kwah or anyone else could recall. He spoke little and even when he did it was more like a series of grunts and gestures than any sort of discernable language. His stature was less giant, closer in size to a large, wide man with long powerful arms. His hair was more like a man's as well, dark and thick on his wide, flat head. He had a full beard and a protruding forehead that coupled with his furry brows served to protect his eyes from the sun. He wore furs most of the time and crude sandals fashioned from multiple layers of homemade leather.

His homeland was geographically close to that of the Red Hairs. Quite alone, he lived in the rocky hills and caves near where The Three set out on their initial voyage. Watching from afar, by means of useful and serviceable intelligence he bought his way onto the boat. He was brilliant with tools and invention and without his help it is said The Reds would have never made the journey to the Americas.

Chapter Three

The Boom

A hundred giants on one side of the field and four hundred men on the other. They all had clubs and were intent on pounding each other to smithereens. The giants win hands down.

Same opponents, only now they have swords, spears, and shields as well as clubs. Giants still win. Introduce bows and arrows into the conversation and all of a sudden a giant victory doesn't seem so certain anymore. Give them all guns and giants fall.

Ironically, the giants of the far east who had the least amount of use for gunpowder were the first to have it. Much like their western cousins, they were peaceful and one with the Earth. But to that extent they were much more. They were monks, priests of the religion of men, held closer to God for their stature, longevity and patience. They wore long robes spun from golden silk and lived among men in mountaintop cathedrals. They were studied and many scrolls of their ancient wisdom were transcribed for the library at Alexandria.

It was their "hand cannons" that eventually found their way onto the decks of ships as swivel guns, for it was the Robed Giants who created the black powder necessary to make them fire. And fire they did as their invention both travelled and bastardized the world.

It was a staple of battlefield warfare at the time for an army to march out their giants. Front and center in order to strike fear into the enemy. The more giants, the better. Heavy and intimidatingly designed armor was sufficient to defeat most of the arrows. With the onset of firearms, giants were nothing more than giant targets who consumed resources and bullied the other soldiers.

Guns turned war giants into 20th century buggy whips, useful only for recreations and nostalgia.

In the American southwest, the Conquistadors first introduced the Red Hairs to gunfire with the arquebus, a slow-loading and firing long gun that made a loud boom and scared primitive enemies. The giants were unimpressed and pummeled the Spanish invaders with large boulders and stones tossed from high rocky outcroppings. A Conquistador's first choice in weapon was generally a sword, followed by a crossbow. The arquebuses were mainly fired as they retreated. They were never known to have killed a giant, and most never even saw what they were shooting at.

With advancements in weapon technology marching ever forward, the Red Hairs soon realized that taking the occasional bullet had painful and sometimes life-ending consequences. Most of the time the giants ended up just carrying them around with them under their skin for the rest of their lives. And almost every giant had one. They became a topic of conversation, almost like a trophy. Hardly did there exist a worthy giant who didn't have at least one bullet stuck in them. Kwah himself had a rather large round lodged just in front of and above his left ear that most just assumed to be a boil.

Embedded weapon fragments were so common in giants that skeletons and mummified remains secretly exhumed by archeologists all had at least one in them, and sometimes many more, including stone arrowheads, so cause of death was naturally assumed. In some cases they were correct, as it was often the last bullet that completed the task.

Aside from the Far East Giants who started the craze, guns and giants did not go hand in hand. As a mass manufactured item, they were simply too small. The enormous fingers of giants could barely pick up an individual bullet, much less fit their fingers into the guard in order to pull the trigger.

Occasionally some snide war lord would let a giant hold a cannon and aim, but the recoil was extensive and burns were common. Often the mismanagement of the weapons took the lives of more of their own men than the enemy's. But there was one who took the practice to a whole new level. The giant known as Bome.

Bome was him saying his own name, mimicking the sound of the cannon he carried. Some thought he was actually saying boom but the bass in his voice was such that it distorted the word. A person could ask him twice if they didn't understand but three times meant possibly irritating Bome, a practice that would likely result in an extremely abbreviated lifespan.

Bome was wide across the shoulders and exceptionally strong. At nearly ten cubits, he was one of the largest of the giants on any battlefield, ever, anywhere. It was thought that he came from Northern Africa or the Middle East. His skin was a dark bronzetone ever painted with soot from cannon fire. He had a patch of black leather over one eye while the other was a starkly contrasting white, like the eight on a billiard ball. His eyebrows were thick and bushy, black and protruding and the long hair on his head was much the same. He wore a bronze helmet turned black and blue from the patina of battle and time.

His armor was a suit of leather, the darkest brown and hard formed. It was thicker than any had ever seen and was said to be ancient, carved from the back of a Mastodon. The evidence was in the hair on the hide, intentionally left as shoulder epaulettes. In Bome's case, the epaulettes helped to cushion the weight of the two cannons he carried.

They were bronze, highly ornate cannons, each weighing as much as two large men and as long as one. During a battle at sea on his initial journey from his homeland, a young giant, unable to swim was willing to do all he could to survive. That included picking up and aiming a cannon at close range boarders. As the battle raged, a trio of sailors would work to load a cannon. Bome would fire it, drop it, and pick up another, fire, and so on. His gun crew were legendary bad men who had to fight for the honor to serve him. There were only two rules - be fast and don't disappoint Bome.

Once firmly on the ground Bome saw no reason to discontinue the practice although gun crewmen became increasingly difficult to find. Between battles, sickness, disease, and being snacked on by other giants, half the time Bome had to load his own guns.

Against all odds Bome was never killed in battle. Instead he became a well-respected elder of the community. He didn't move much and said even less. The thick, black hair turned gray and most didn't think he could stand up straight anymore. A peaceful place to relax in the forest is just what Bome had in mind for his retirement. He was calmed by the presence of so many trees.

They moved at night in small groups so as not to attract too much attention. It's hard to sneak when your very footsteps shake the ground but giants were exceptionally light on their feet for their weight. They also had an excellent sense of smell and needed not see each other in order to follow another's scent. They really may have been able to smell the blood of an Englishman, suggesting the nursery rhyme wasn't entirely false after all.

The giants chose the basalt cliffs along the St Croix River to carve out their home. On top they would grow what they could and store it in the off season in cool air caves dug out with huge pick axes. The water was clean and plentiful and the river had a hard bottom that would thwart drowning. The few Vibrant Oxen that survived the journey would be farmed as cattle in the natural plains just inland of the river.

Individual homes were pits dug out from rock and sand with roofs of heavy pine logs covered by dirt and moss. Each had a hearth for warmth and cooking with chimneys made from slabs of stone. From a distance, together they looked like a smoking graveyard that most humans dare not approach.

They helped each other build initially, as the journey was one of like-minded solidarity. No more wars, no more fighting to stay alive. They just wanted to be left alone, to exist. No longer would they slaughter and eat humans. Instead they would trade with them, learn to live with them, but from afar.

Once word spread in the giant community, they came from all over, to build, to live in peace. If you were a giant, and you were not there, then you were alone. It was as simple as that. From the outside looking in, including the men who paid attention to such things, it looked very much like they were building an army.

Native war chiefs of the local tribes held council to discuss their options, putting aside their own discord to avoid perceived annihilation. It was decided they would meet with the giants in order to discover their intent.

The youngest chief, an Ojibwe from the north and seven other brave men approached the settlement. Aside from a trickle of smoke from a few of the chimneys the village appeared empty and there was some confusion amongst the men. They called out but received no answer.

As they stepped together toward the entry of the first abode they encountered, a loud, low moan took over the air around them, the vibrations shook their chests. The ground beneath them trembled and bulged, forcing them backwards with their focus on whatever was about to break through before them.

Two cannons came through the turf held aloft on the shoulders of the feared giant Bome. Bome himself had been thrust upwards by two other giants beneath him. Behind them in order to thwart their retreat, the men backed into a wall of giants dressed for war. Giants whom they never heard approaching as their focus and fear was clearly elsewhere. The giants roared in unison as the native men fell to their knees holding their palms tightly over their ears.

"Enough," Kwah said, his feet pounding out his theatrical approach.

He picked up one of the men with his left arm only and shook him until he dropped his weapons. After which he tossed him to the ground. He did the same to the next man and as he approached the third looked him squarely in the eyes expecting him to drop his weapons on his own, which he did, which all the remaining men did, and quickly.

Kwah motioned for the smallest giant, he of unknown ancestry to gather the weapons as he was the most skilled among them concerning dexterity and tools. Bome leaned in, inches from the chief, his nose as big as the chief's entire face. He sniffed him hard, as if checking on dinner in a pot on the stove. Bome's foul breath borne of rotten teeth caused the chief to grimace and repel. This pleased Bome and by all accounts, this was a good thing.

Giants had two rows of teeth, one behind the other and unlike humans, two sets of spares buried in their skull waiting to replace the rotted ones that would have jumped out and ran away if they could. Not a giant alive had ever heard of brushing them.

"Gaawiin onji," Kwah said. In Ojibwe. "No fight."

"Bekaadesiwin, peace."

With the summit a new peace was born between giants and men. Native men at least. Besides the occasional trapper or wayward lost explorer, white men were few and far between. It would be some time before they spread across the wilderness, and spread they did, from east to west, from south to north they came. And once they arrived, a whole new understanding would have to be met.

Unfortunately for the giants, they were not used to the greed and determination of these men and women. It had been since Roman Times that they knew men such as these, vaguely recalling stories spun by elders who were long gone to the wind. These people were different. They were born to take, to use, to gain, and they would not be deterred.

Chapter Four

Goetz the Gold

1830's Wisconsin Territory. Europeans were expanding their range, moving west of the Great Lakes in search of natural resources to exploit. The rich were fully intent on getting richer at the expense of the environment and poor men. Immense forests of towering White Pine many hundreds of years old stood sentinel on both sides of the upper St. Croix River seemingly ad infinitum. The goal was to harvest every last one and Horace Goetz was just the man for the job.

New England had enough of him, or more accurately, Horace Goetz had enough of New England. There wasn't much more Horace could borrow, beg, or steal. Horace's grandfather fought the Redcoats in the Revolution earning him the opportunity to tag along to Louisiana in 1814. Horace wasn't the sort to pick up a gun by any means but supplies can be difficult to procure, especially if they are not issued by the army. The army needed men of his ilk, soulless purveyors of all things non-issued. Anything and everything for a price. Even his superior officers would use his conniving unscrupulousness to circumvent red tape and the occasional order to achieve victories that may not have otherwise been possible without his help. Regardless of his low moral character, Horace's patriotism could never be questioned.

Early in 1836 Horace headed north, quickly. Rumor has it he became a rich man in a relatively short amount of time. Some say he came through New Mexico but such a journey through the untamed wilderness seemed unlikely to be successful for a man of his stature. Those same people claimed he met with Santa Anna and could barely carry his gold back across the border.

Goetz himself declared he made out well on a temporary gold mine partnership after the strike in Georgia a few years earlier. After selling his share he simply "decided to embark on a different challenge" as everything else was just too easy for him.

After a year in Chicago selling and trading goods and services through ports across the Great Lakes, Goetz once again was hastily forced to vacate the area for reasons unknown, although wealthier and somewhat wiser.

Goetz arrived in the Stillwater area by riverboat in late spring of 1838 when the winter meltwaters began to recede. It is widely accepted that he jumped ship once the boat he was on turned towards Fort Snelling in St. Paul wanting nothing to do with the U.S. Army. Although he most definitely switched boats prior to the confluence of the St. Croix and the Mississippi, he was known to carry a lot of gold so it was unlikely he would have been able to physically navigate the current.

Stillwater was as implied. A good place on the river to turn such a boat, refuel, and retire one's self from the rigors of boat life. There was a log trading post, hotel, saloon, and a general store. A smattering of houses and barns stretched up the hillside peeking out from trees like children playing games. Stick built skeletons of buildings in process lined both sides of the future main street. Some of the land was cleared but most not yet.

In leu of brick and mortar, miscellaneous vendors set up shop along the route in canvas tents pitched in the mud selling everything from lumber to beaver pelts. The air was foul from livestock. Nothing liquid runs uphill, especially in this town.

The dock was mighty, able to accommodate many boats, running it's girth parallel to the shore instead of jutting out like a nail through the backside of a board. Once both his feet were firmly in place upon it, Horace arched his back, threw out his chest and marveled at all that was around him, spinning and dancing in circles.

Two days later Goetz assumed ownership of the newest building in town. Later that summer he opened up the First Bank of Stillwater. By the fall of 1838 he commissioned a new bank to be built the following spring, a building of brick and mortar further up the hill. He was known to urinate in the road in front of the bank as a sort of payback for the scent of the livestock below. This was generally done after hours and under the influence. Goetz denied that this ever happened, even while buttoning his trousers and walking away.

"This is no way to run a town," Goetz was often heard saying while standing on the balcony of the old bank building.

Horace was disgusted by the farm animals living in and so close to town. He made it his own personal quest to see that they were removed permanently. When asked why a man as wealthy as himself did not just buy the farmers out of their land he responded, "Why would I? I would do well to make them pay me."

Horace Goetz was a thin man, rather tall with a pale, almost sickly complexion. The jawline of his sunken, raw-boned face could cut a steak. One tuft of hair as wide as a pen and half the length grew from his ball-shaped chin. His hairline, receding, in his youth was jet black but as of late more salt than pepper. It did not really matter because he was not seen outside his home without his signature black bowler. It matched his eyes which due to his atypically large pupils appeared black as well. Black coat, black pants, black army boots, and a white shirt.

Terminally single, Goetz preferred ladies of the night, readily available at the saloon he opened in the building that used to be the bank. Gambling, prostitution, and bad manners were constants, but they served the best steak in town. In order to maximize his profits, Goetz needed cows.

There were three different farms that were abutting and in some cases, part of the town. Goetz met with all three farmers convincing them it was in their best interest to raise cows.

"The future is bright. Many will need to be fed!" Goetz told them.

All three farmers had at least one cow each but lacked the money and infrastructure necessary to make a large scale operation work.

"May I propose a partnership? I will provide the funding necessary to expand for half ownership of your farm, even if the cost is more than half the worth. In return I will buy beef at cost until the debt is paid. Interest free. After that date you shall be sole owner of your farm again and I shall buy at ten percent below market in perpetuity as rent for my wealth. Agreed?" Horace asked.

It was too good of a deal for the men to say no. The three farms grew at an exceptional rate on land purchased by Goetz. Many new outbuildings were constructed, their locations and construction managed entirely by Goetz, who demanded final approval of all projects before the bills would be paid.

"It don't make no sense though, Horace. You got one a going this way, and another way over yonder facing to the south. Mueller and Housen told me the same thing is goin' on over at their places," the Farmer complained.

"It makes perfect sense. Once it is all complete it will become most obvious to you," Goetz explained.

What happened next started as a murmur half spoken through a whiskey bottle and ended as a scream. Gold.

Goetz had the evidence in his hands, handfuls of the cleanest gold nuggets anyone had ever seen.

"Where'd they come from? Where'd you git 'em?" the townspeople demanded.

"I am not at liberty to discuss. The owner wishes to remain anonymous," Goetz said officially. "All I can tell you is that he's local," he would then whisper.

And so began the Great Stillwater gold rush of 1840. Goetz was prepared. He built hotels. Complete with modern saloons and restaurants. He built a creamery and hired chefs from Chicago who were thrilled to work with so much fresh dairy and beef.

The three farmers demanded a meeting for a serious grievance.

"Horace, you done takin' so much of the beef we ain't gonna have none left for market. We got bills to pay. You know on the land, grain, well you know Horace, you know what it cost," they said.

"I can assure you gentlemen that I will gladly cover my half of the bank payment. If you fail to meet your obligations I am sorry to inform you that you will be in default. I cannot manage your money for you after all, you're grown men," Horace said snidely and then had them removed by the sheriff he appointed.

The existing farms were vacated and the remaining cows were transferred to a newly cleared farm two miles west of town. This farm would be managed for hire with hands sharing the gracious residence, owned in its entirety by Horace Goetz, or more accurately, H.G. Incorporated. The old fences were removed and a grid of dirt roads carved into the abandoned fields. Roads that very conveniently lined up perfectly with the buildings Goetz had erected during the initial farm expansions.

The three farmers paid out all they had and left town in debt.

"They should be in prison," Goetz said. "We ought build one."

More fortune would befall Goetz as he very wisely invested in a store that provided mining equipment to the general public. And as much of the land that used to be part of the three farms was occupied by rocky hills and bluffs, it was Mr. Goetz's pleasure to split it into claims available on a first come, first serve cash basis, sans any promises of gold. The miscellaneous number of nuggets Goetz scattered and buried in the rocks and streams were nothing more than a cost of doing business compared to the money he netted off the sale of the land he stole.

As bad luck would have it, nobody else struck it rich. When the stink eye turned towards Horace, he was ready. He introduced the sacked investors to a new deal, a new scheme that could make them money, possibly enough to recoup their investments. Sell their lumber to him and he would pay them to take it to the mill. By the time they returned, he would procure more land on which to harvest trees. He would pay them a fair wage and the company would build grand houses on the land they themselves already owned. Together they would build a town and a future.

Goetz offered to build a school and hire a doctor for the town. Stores would be brimming with fresh food and free churches would be erected for the general welfare and decency of the people. With so much given, all Goetz requested in return was a reduction of market wages but at a far lesser rate than if a man would have to pay for all these things on his own.

Finally, elections would be held for Mayor and Sherriff so the people of Stillwater will know that no one man is above any other.

Two men died on the initial raft of logs floated downriver to the nearest mill, their homes never built, their abandoned lands reclaimed by the bank. Those who returned built, lived and survived in one of the first company towns in the nation.

The Panic of 1837 was a nationwide financial crisis that resulted in a recession that lasted well into the 1840's. Men around the country did whatever they had to in order to hop a river boat and be a part of the town of Stillwater. The promise of a home for their families and steady work was more than most men could hope for at the time, regardless of the wage.

Horace Goetz had every piece in place in order to win the game except one thing, trees. Goetz needed standing timber, a lot of it. For that he needed land and for that he needed the U.S. Government to modify their treaty with the native nations. When asked why he didn't just buy the timber rights from the natives outright he replied, "Why would I? I would do well to make them pay me."

Chapter Five

Giiwanimo

Streaked with dried mud, a small blonde-haired girl in a long cotton dressed screamed blue bloody murder, running from the river as if the water was on fire.

It was common for sawed logs from the rafts headed towards the mills to break away and lodge against the shoreline. Kids used them to build docks for fishing or for rolling games when the water temperature permitted.

It was a Tuesday morning in early June when three such logs tied together to form a raft with ivy vines wedged itself into the sand where the children played along the shoreline. On top of the small raft were six parts of a man, separated and neatly tied on board so as not to fall off into the river.

Especially horrific upon further examination by the town doctor was the man had been literally torn limb from limb.

"Here, look at the clothes, they tore right along with him," the doctor said.

"Where's Horace? This is one of his guys," the Sherrif said.

"*Was* one of his guys," another man said, attempting to add some cold-hearted levity to the situation. Usually drunk and always crass, this man was the kind not to be left alone around children, especially female children.

The doctor took off his coat and laid it over what could be covered of the deceased. By this time word had spread around town and a group of people were headed towards the river.

"Who is it?"

"Who would do this?"

"Do what?"

"What happened?" the collective asked.

"It was Indians for sure," the crass man yelled out, stirring up the crowd. "I seent some yesterday eyein' up the young ins. They had that look. You know, like they was gonna be up to somethin' hadn't I come along. Damn savages," the man said, adding fuel to the fire.

The crowd took the bait and the formerly low hum of confusion became a rallying cry of discord amongst the easily manipulated populace.

"Let's go get em' and hang em'," the crass man then demanded as they were now on the verge of being completely out of control.

At that moment a shot rang out and everything went quiet besides the echo. The crass man fell forward into the mud, a bullet hole in the back of his skull. Horace Goetz was still holding his pistol at arm's length where the accusatory man had been formerly standing. The sheriff, with his hand on the butt of the pistol still in his holster did nothing while the doctor reached down and put his index finger in the bullet hole.

"It is my professional opinion that this man, distraught over finding his friend in such a state most obviously committed suicide. Wouldn't you agree sheriff?" the doctor asked.

The crowd, now silent besides a few low tones backed away and formed a circle around Horace and the dead man. The sheriff never did answer the question.

"The hell he did," Horace said indignantly.

"This man worked for me. His name was Tyler Howard. He had no family that I know of. I considered him a friend but he would not have died for me. Return to your homes. I assure you I will get to the bottom of this," Horace told the crowd.

"Who amongst your enemies might draw and quarter a man?" the doctor asked Horace.

"This man was not drawn and quartered," Goetz replied.

"How do you know?" the sheriff asked.

Goetz looked annoyed that he was being forced to explain himself to those whom he considered lessor.

"Ain't seen too many Romans around these parts. How 'bout you? And contrary to what you've heard or might believe, Indians don't kill a man like this. That ain't nothin' but folklore. And even if they did, they'd have to use ropes. Look close. No burns. And no way ropes, or chains, or whatever they used would tear the clothes like this," Horace explained as he walked away.

"Where you going Goetz?" the sheriff asked. "What are we supposed to do with him?"

"Bury him" Goetz said. "Or at least what's left of him."

"And him?" the sheriff asked referring to the crass man.

Goetz thought on it for a matter of seconds before motioning with his head towards the river. "Kick him in. Meet me back at the office directly."

Back at his office in the second floor of the bank building, Horace held a glass of neat whiskey and stared out at the town through distorted glass windows.

"Have a seat Klien," Goetz ordered.

Goetz met Maribel Klein on his journey north by river years prior. Klein lit out towards Fort Snelling while Goetz continued up the St. Croix. Onboard they developed a relationship where Klein, a seemingly normal man propped Goetz up on some sort of pseudo god pedestal. Goetz was the bulldog and Klien was the little mutt that hopped alongside.

Once Goetz had the reins of the town firmly in hand, he sent for Klein and appointed him sheriff.

What made the relationship more peculiar was that Klien did not appear to be a simple man. He was quite the opposite and far from a coward. He was rather large framed for the times, stayed cleanshaven, kept his black hair short, and dressed neatly. He also wore a bowler although considerably larger than Goetz's and never in black.

"He wasn't alone," Goetz said.

"Who? Tyler?" Klien asked.

"Yes. You think I care about the other vermin? Of course Tyler, I sent four men, men you know, into the wilderness, leaving behind wives and children. They were to survey, to scout new stands of lumber, work out the details of the cut so to speak," Goetz explained.

"But now, after seeing what whoever or whatever did to Tyler I suspect we will surely know more widows." Goetz took a long drag from his cigar and blasted it upward, watching the smoke dissipate into the room.

"In the morning I want every man we can spare mounted and ready. Not sure how long we'll be out so pack heavy. We head north, they would have stayed on the west side so that's where we'll go but I want a small party on the east side as well. They can cross upstream. Get some men and go door to door. Everyone come to the hotel in the morning and we'll leave as soon as we have enough men," Goetz instructed.

Goetz, Klien, and a group of over twenty men rode up the west side of the river two abreast, while a much smaller group of four rode the east side. At times the trails along the bluffs were either too narrow or too steep and the horses had to walk one behind the other. Goetz never rode lead, choosing instead to stay back so that he wouldn't catch the first bullet.

The first day was uneventful. The smaller group crossed a half day's ride north of town where the river narrowed. No man on either side happened across any person living or dead before nightfall. The men yelled back and forth at each other in the darkness as each group could see the flicker of the other camp's fire.

"Idiots," Horace grumbled.

Day two would prove to be far more eventful as the sun had barely been above the trees before they came upon a man and woman in camp along the west shoreline.

"Hey in camp!" Klien yelled down.

The group was riding along the top of the bluff while the man was panning for gold in the gravel along the shoreline. He had the look of a stereotypical prospector, or maybe a trapper. The pans and the pelts in his camp told the tale of both.

"Hello up there!" the prospector yelled back while his wife slapped him on the back as punishment.

"What? They already know we're here," he snapped at her.

As four of the men, Klien and Goetz, and two others made their way down the hill through the woods the woman yelled.

"Awas, awas!"

"She says go away," the prospector translated.

"An Indian woman. Where'd you get her?" Goetz asked.

"You got it all wrong mister. She got me. I guess you could say early on, right away like, I was captivated by her beauty," he said smiling a nearly toothless grin.

"We're looking for some men. Would of came through here, oh, maybe three, four days ago. Four of them. Say. What's your name stranger?" Goetz asked.

The prospector hesitated, bewildered momentarily he broke out in a laugh.

"Funny, ain't heard nobody say it in so long I done nearly forgot it. Elsenpeter, Roy," he said.

"Roy Elsenpeter have you seen my men?" Goetz asked pointedly.

"Um, no, no. I ain't seen anyone," he said while shying away, poking the coals of the nearby fire.

"What about her?" Goetz asked motioning to Roy's wife. "The Indian woman."

"Ina'adoo agaami bemaadzid mishi amo mishi," she said angrily.

"Oh, uh, well, she said she ain't seen no one like that neither. Ok then, you boys have a good day then," Roy stammered.

To Goetz, it was obvious that none of his companions could speak Ojibwe. If they had, they might have turned around.

"We ride on then, north," Goetz commanded.

"Wait a minute. I say he's lyin' I know it when I see it. I got some questions for you mister," Klien said.

"No, we ride on I said! I believe him. What's more is I believe her," Goetz said.

Roy looked at him sideways, grabbed Goetz's saddle and leaned in close. "You understood her? And you still wanna go?"

Goetz leaned down to listen but sat upright again without breaking eye contact. He also chose to not respond.

Three of the men set back up the tree covered bluff while Goetz stayed back momentarily.

"Say what you must old man. Tell me more of these giants," he said.

"They ain't men. Don't nobody go there. Not even her people, 'cept for gifts but they don't go in," Roy explained.

"Go in where? Where are these 'giants'?" Goetz asked.

Elsenpeter walked away, refusing to answer but stopped mid-gait when Goetz clicked the hammer back on his pistol.

"I will shoot her first," Goetz said pointing his gun at the woman.

"Okay, okay, don't say I didn't warn ya. You're gonna' start seeing things, things that don't quite make sense. You're gonna wonder how things got to where they are, boulders, deadfalls and such. Bout that time they gonna be across the river and more than likely they already gonna know you're there. Mister, if your men went up there then I highly doubt they ever comin' back. And same for you," Roy explained.

"How do you know about them, how do you know where they are? What I'm going to see? You look to be the better part of alive to me. How did you get through?" Goetz asked sidestepping his horse closer to Roy's wife while training the gun on her forehead.

"Okay, please. Now I don't know for sure but according to her people you gotta give 'em something. Something they can use. Food if ya got it, that's what she done told me. You try leavin' a feather or somethin' like that and they'll likely kill you on the spot. Make 'em mad," Roy said.

'Mister Goetz? You okay down there?" Klien yelled from the brush above.

"Fine, fine. Be up directly," Goetz yelled back.

Goetz holstered his pistol, turned his horse and walked away, stopping for one last question.

"By the way, you find any gold?" he asked.

"Nope, sure as hell not a spec. The fella that done said there's gold around here ought be shot ifin ya ask me," Roy said.

"Careful Mr. Elsenpeter. The man just might shoot back," he said.

Goetz spun around on his horse and shot Roy in the center of his heart. His wife screamed in terror as she dove forward to catch his fall.

"Giiwanimo, he lies!" Goetz chided as he rode back up the bluff.

Chapter Six

Posse Comitatus

"Now how in the heck?" Klien asked.

The posse came to a halt in order to take in a very unnatural phenomenon. High in the pines, possibly more than forty feet above the ground, the trunk of another large tree was tied in place horizontally between two others.

"It don't make no sense," Klien said.

"No, maybe not. But those vines sure do look familiar." Goetz was referring to the vines used to tie the trunk in place. They were of the same type used to lash the log raft that carried Tyler's body parts into the bay.

On the east side, the smaller group found oddities of their own, also defying explanation. Five logs stood on end to form a teepee but without covering. The logs were heavy and long. Atop the cradle where they intersected was perched a large, roundish boulder similar in size to a bathtub. The logs were not tied at the top and disturbing one of them meant the boulder would fall in a random direction. This was one of five such structures the group found built in a line at the edge of a large field.

"What in God's green earth is that?" the rider asked.

On the far edge of the field was an animal unlike anything any of the men had seen before. They had all seen oxen before, horses pulling plows had only just recently become the go to animals for the job as they were easier to work with and served dual purpose. These oxen were clearly different. Nearly twice the height of a man at the shoulders and wider than a wagon, the horns would not allow them to walk through any forest in the country. They were also decidedly not brown, instead sporting the vibrant colors for which they were named.

The men in their defense had never heard of a Vibrant Ox and they also did not know that the oxen had such excellent hearing. When they heard the men talking, they became curious.

"I think they heard us. Hell, I think they're a comin'," a rider said nervously.

A Vibrant Ox is a curious creature, very docile outside of breeding season they fear nothing. Animals their size have no real natural predators. This is one of the reasons they evolved with such bright colors and the ability to see them. They did not have much use for night vision like regular oxen that trades nighttime clarity for a black, white and gray existence. Sneaking up on them wouldn't do much good for a courageous predator anyway considering their immensity and armor plating.

Reproduction success for Vibrants is low and their colors help to attract mates from great distances across open plains. Growing even a moderate sized herd can take many years, equivalent to a long lifetime of a human being.

The men on the east side were not privy to this information and when two of the Vibrants began to run straight for their position, they thought it best to open fire. It was likely the oxen didn't even know they were being hit by bullets until they closed within less than a hundred yards. Once they grew extremely close, they realized what was happening immediately and halted their charge. Two of the men stopped firing as they perceived emotion from the oxen who looked to the men as if their feelings were genuinely hurt, complete with sad oxen frowns. Two of the men saw things differently and continued to fire.

"They just bouncin' off, ain't even hurting them," one of the men yelled over the gunfire.

"Aim for the eyes," the other said.

This prompted a response from the oxen who in unison bellowed out what was known to the giants as "the roar of a thousand shofar." A shofar is an ancient instrument made from a ram's horn and used as a bugle. A bugle that could be heard miles away.

One of the men still firing turned out to be a fine shot. They had unwittingly discovered one of the very few weaknesses of the Vibrant Ox, a bullet's path to the brain. The first caused the beast to sit back on its haunches, hence the time of the roar. The second shot, same eye, killed it dead. The other ox ran back the way it came sounding like a slow talking Santa Claus with an extra deep 'Ho'.

"Look at this fellas. Ain't nobody gonna believe us. Hell each side of the horns could wrap around my horse," one of the men said, dismounting for a closer look.

The field was as wide as a lake, too far for a man to make out detail on the other side. It was precisely the other side from where they heard the 'sound'.

"Nooooo!"

It wasn't overly thunderous but loud enough that they could hear it. It was deep, and low, nearly subsonic. They felt it as much as they heard it. After some discussion they couldn't even agree on what the noise even was. Some heard "no" but the longer they thought about it, the more indetermined the answer was. Unanimously they decided to investigate and besides, it was on the way.

Continuing on the west side, further down the trail from the suspended log, the larger posse came across a deadfall trap of such considerable size that it had them all questioning reality.

"I believe if there had been a plate of meat on the end of that thing I dare say one of us would be dead for sure," one of the men said.

"It's a Paiute. Seen 'em before. Not this big though. Not sure I can work out how they were able to set this, much less lift the stone," Goetz said.

Paiute deadfalls are one of the oldest known of these types of traps, designed primarily for small game and rodents. They consisted of a trigger stick, a lever stick, a bait stick, bait and a flat stone. When the bait is taken, the stone falls killing the animal. This particular trap had sticks as wide as a man's thigh and a flat stone that likely weighed many tons.

The trail was wide here and the slope to the river was gentle through the forest. The river rippled before them, suggesting shallower water with a hard, rocky bottom. The posse took notice of distant gunshots and what could only be described as a giant tuba or a horn prompting them to ride to the river post haste. They waited intently to hear anything else that might help them understand what was happening while the horses drank the clean, cool water. They heard nothing.

"I say we head over there. What say you Mr. Goetz?" one of the men asked.

Goetz looked the area over closely, including a detailed scan of the bluffs behind them.

"I say we wait. Those shots were some distance away. Now that they have ceased, one would guess that they either have killed whatever they were shooting at, or have been killed by it, making any urgency on our part moot," Goetz explained.

Some time had passed before they heard anything more, long enough for some of the men to grab some shuteye in the shade. Shots rang out once more but this time close enough that they were mixed with audible shouting, the details of which were impossible to determine.

After the echo of the last shot dissipated, there came a deafening silence. Hails from the posse went unanswered and concern among the men grew quickly.

"I say we head over now. This is as good of a place as any. If it be injuns, there ain't gonna be enough of them to take us guaranteed. What say you Mr. Goetz?" the same man asked again.

Goetz looked around once again and this time agreed with the man. "Yes, I do believe that would be the proper coarse of action given the circumstances."

"Okay then let's go boys!" the rider yelled.

Goetz tugged on the back of Klien's sleeve and shook his head 'no', signaling that he wished for him to stay behind.

The emotional posse advanced through the river carefully at first, picking up speed as they passed the midway point. They did not notice that Goetz and Klien did not ride along. By the time they reached the opposite shore, they were shouting, splashing, and dashing towards the perceived danger. Each and every one of them intent on being heroes. Mere moments later, the shooting began.

"I gotta get over there," Klien said.

"I wouldn't do that if I were you. If I'm correct, and I usually am, who, or rather what those men are facing is a nightmare from which they will not wake up," Goetz said.

The posse charged up the trail out of the river side by side. It was rocky and steep without much vegetation. The first giant stepped out from behind the cliff's edge and wrapped each hand around the necks of the first two horses in line. He spun a backwards pirouette with the horses, riders still mounted and hanging on for dear life. Like a sort of spinning saw he advanced into the rest of the riders, clubbing them to smithereens with the flailing hooves and bodies of the large animals.

Men who were able fired their weapons which seemed to annoy him further. Another giant with long black hair like the first appeared with a club carved from an ancient pine, larger around than a whiskey barrel at the business end. Each blow whether striking man or beast ended that particular life.

Within mere minutes the battle was over. Of the twenty three-men who crossed the river, five survived the initial attack. The survivors suffered injuries ranging from broken bones to internal bleeding. Huddled together and now surrounded by giants they could do nothing but fear their deaths.

Klien was removed from his horse with such force and speed that he had no real idea in the world what was happening to him. Goetz only had time to turn around and although he had to swallow a whole imaginary orange in one gulp, he wasn't completely surprised to be staring up at the face of a giant. Sheriff Klien was. They never heard him coming.

Kwah held Klien horizontally with two hands.

"Who are you? Or I tear him in two," Kwah said.

"Please large sir, we mean you no harm," Goetz said after which he removed his pistol and tossed it on the ground.

Kwah watched him do so and switching Klien to one hand, the giant glared at him nose to nose until he did the same as Goetz and threw down his weapons. He was only happy to comply.

Kwah tossed him to the side and shook his hand as if wet.

"Stink. Yours?" Kwah asked pointing to where the posse crossed.

"Yes." Goetz said.

"Yours?" Kwah asked again only this time pointing into the distance at where the other group encountered the ox.

"Um, I'm not exactly sure what you mean?" Goetz said.

He knew exactly what the giant meant but he did not want to be held responsible for variables to which he was not privileged to be aware of.

"Your men kill my ox," Kwah said.

"Sir I can assure you…," Goetz was interrupted by Kwah's huge voice before he could finish his thought.

"Your men!" Kwah yelled. "Kill my ox. We'll keep them fresh. Eat ox now, men later. Things are quiet now. All your men dead. You could be dead. Leave now and tell others to stay away. Leave us to be. No more men come to take trees," Kwah told them.

"Thank you mighty giant sir. We will do as you ask but before we leave as we are obviously no threat to you might I ask a question?" Goetz asked boldly.

Kwah only sighed and collapsed his shoulders. He knew he would have to deal with men eventually but was not looking forward to it.

"If food is an issue, I would ask you and yours if you have eaten beef? A cow for example would be beef," Goetz stated. "See the thing is I am the one who a man would go back and tell, the man in charge so to speak. That puts me in the unique position to maybe broker a deal. An agreement if you will. The fact is my people are many, and we need lumber, trees, wood."

Kwah took an angry step towards Goetz who put both hands out defensively.

"Now, now that doesn't mean your trees per se'. Other trees, away from here. Trees you could cut and send downriver. My men will collect them and send them together the rest of the way. For your troubles I will supply you with beef, a lot of beef in fact. Brought to you on the hoof. You kill and eat them whenever you like. You will never be short of food again, even in the coldest winters. Do you have a leader, someone who could make that decision?" Goetz asked.

"I am the one a giant would go back and tell," Kwah said imposingly.

Chapter Seven

Jammed

"What about the men?" Klien asked.

"They are dead, and there is nothing we can do about that now," Goetz said. "We can only help ourselves or we will surely join them."

"If I understood the details, we're going to need some bigger saws," Klien said as he and Goetz rode back to town.

"Correct. There is to be no contact. Leave them at the first marker. They will send word when they are ready," Goetz explained.

"How?"

"Apparently they have an intermediary they sometimes use," Goetz said.

"Who?"

"We will know her as Sky Dancer or Sky for short. She will be ahead down this very trail at a camp with her husband whom I more than strongly suspect to be Mr. Roy Elsenpeter and yes I very much am aware of the irony," Goetz said.

"She don't speak no English though. Why choose a go-between that don't speak English? Don't make no sense," Klien said.

"They didn't choose her to go-between them and us," Goetz explained.

They found Sky at the camp setting the final stones over her husband. There was no marker, no cross, only heavy stones covering a shallow, makeshift grave mound head to toe.

She expected that if they lived, they would be back. She wondered how many there would be, and how she could kill them, especially him. Her stomach dropped roller-coaster style when she saw only two, including him. Her only fear was that he might die too quickly.

"Now, now, wait a minute, hold on there," Goetz said with his hands in the air.

Sky had a rifle in her hands and was in the process of raising it to her shoulder.

"We are here on behalf of the giant Kwah," he said.

She lowered the weapon and shook it in frustration.

"Hey, seems like she understood you," Klein said.

"She understands English, just doesn't speak it," Goetz said. He spoke down to her from atop his horse. She stared back at him, cold, teeth clenched in hatred. "There'll be men coming through here with supplies. When Kwah tells you, come to town, the bank, ask for me, Horace Goetz. Say it out loud so I know you understand. Go ahead now say it."

Sky refused to udder his name, spitting on the ground in front of him instead.

"Well I guess that's good enough. I suspect you'll remember who I am," Goetz said turning his horse back towards the trail to town.

"How do we know she's gonna do it?" Klien asked.

"Duty. She does it for her people, for peace with the giants because she said she would. It's just that simple for them. As far as she's concerned, we could all be dead," Goetz said.

The decidedly non-triumphant return to town did not go unnoticed. Neither Goetz nor Klien answered any of the questions hollered by townsfolk who were curious as to the state of their loved ones. The men's silence spoke volumes.

The two rode directly to the jail, where there was also an available livery, and locked themselves inside.

"What are we gonna tell them?" Klien asked.

Within moments wives, cousins, grandmothers, and sisters pounded on the heavily fortified front doors of the jail while whores looked on from the balcony across the street.

"We'll tell them the truth. Rogue Indians. You and I riding out front were taken prisoner and tied in a gang with other slaves. Our men mounted a valiant rescue attempt. The Indian girl to whom we were tied was able to drag a man from his saddle and the three of us, unarmed, absconded to safety. Unfortunately outnumbered ten to one our brave men met an untimely demise," Goetz explained.

"But we don't have hardly a mark on us, between the two of us," Klien noticed.

"Yes, about that," Goetz said retrieving a small, coiled section of rope hanging on the peg behind the door.

"Oh and this," Goetz picked up a knife with a short blade, less than three inches long and lodged it into the left shoulder of the sheriff while placing his other hand over Klien's mouth to muffle the scream.

"Tie that off, make sure there's blood on it, wrists too. Now hit me," Goetz demanded.

Klein being a large man thought he might do too much damage if he struck him with too much force so he laid off the first punch.

"Dammit man. A man of your size? No wonder you allow yourself to be led by the reigns," Goetz chided as Klien hit him again, only harder.

Goetz recoiled, the punch hard enough to spin him in place.

"Come now Klien, I will ask the Indian girl next time, she is clearly stronger than you."

The next punch broke open Goetz's lip and bloodied his nose, likely breaking it as well. He blacked out, falling to the ground crimping his neck up against the wall.

"How's that you son-of-a-" Klien contained himself having been satisfied with the results of the last punch.

At the dry sink along the wall he slowly filled the large porcelain bowl with water, relishing in the moment. He doused Goetz bringing him back to the land of the conscious.

"How about we let 'em in?" Klien said.

Goetz could only nod his approval while he stroked his numb jaw. The sheriff unbolted the door and the people poured in.

The scene unfolded as expected. Cries of grief and wailing disbelief fueled by denial and anger. Those who would stay would be helped along by the company with food and housing. Those who did not believe the official recounting of the incident were to be quietly moved from town.

Men who did not partake in the initial posse claimed blood right revenge for their fallen brothers, as well as some of the male children who were old enough to ride.

"Your time will come soon enough my brothers. Together we will ride with the hounds of hell before us, leading the way straight to the gates of hell. Vengeance shall be ours!" Goetz declared, fist held high.

As the crowd dispersed Goetz stopped them with an add-on to his speech.

"People of Stillwater. The Indian girl, the dear brave Indian girl who saved the sheriff and myself, due to her natural fear of men such as us took flight the moment we managed to cut ourselves free. If by chance she is ever seen I believe she will answer to the name Sky. Bring her directly to me. The girl is a hero and needs to be treated as such. Now go back to your homes, send letters to men you know that they are needed, to build, to fight, to claim this country back from the heathens who have killed so many of us today. For a time we will mourn, and we will pray for a greater future, and victory!" he shouted, drawing cheers from a majority of the crowd.

Men did come, from St. Paul, from Milwaukee, from Chicago. They came from out east and from down south. Some came to log, some came to kill, all came to prosper. Goetz wasted no time putting them to work on a boom site north of town.

A boom, or a weir, is a line of logs chained together across the river to catch other floating logs on their way down stream. Here they would be sorted, rafted together and claimed before they could finish their journey to the various mills.

Goetz, while sending men to build the boom, also had a large crew constructing a mill on the north end of town to further enhance his profits. Even more men were sent across the river to the massive natural grass plains to the north. There they were to build fences, water holes, farm steads and outbuildings catered solely to the raising of livestock.

"No man, woman, or child shall hunger while in my employ," Goetz would say often.

The farm was where the cowboys lived, rough and hardy men who cherished a hard life and a good fight. This is where the men who came for blood would land, impatiently tasking until they got their chance to kill Indians. It was common for Native Americans to disappear around the farm.

Once the boom was in place and manned, the first load of super-sized two-giant saws were dropped off at the first marker. One wagon of saws, one wagon load of bread, and six cows were left under the log suspended horizontally high in the trees. Klien himself led the expedition. Three days later Sky walked unassumingly into town not having the slightest idea of what she was in for.

"Look, it's her! Where? Her? Over there! Somebody get Goetz!" they cried.

A crowd surrounded her, asking her questions, digging to test rumors that the story Goetz told was not true. She spoke only in her own tongue and the people did not understand. Collectively they steered her to the bank. Goetz came out onto the balcony to the sounds of so much ruckus.

"There she is! My hero! Please, won't you come in?" he asked gesturing for her to enter.

As much as she was enjoying the onslaught of praise and admiration, her heart fell below the water line when she looked up and saw Goetz there, smiling, standing above so many others.

After a short meeting the two stepped out front where Goetz once again gave a speech.

"Anything this young woman needs she shall have. Our best room, the finest food and drink. She will be granted free passage to any place at any time. Her name is Sky, and she will report directly to me. No harm is to ever befall her. She will help us. The enemy hides, they are deceitful and without moral compass or courage. We must think like an Indian, to catch an Indian. Furthermore, as some of you have heard, we have camps in the north, many men who wait for the chance to war with the bloodthirsty heathens. These men have begun to cut back the forest. To take away from them who we must kill in order to guarantee our own survival. Soon, our mills will be full, as will be our purses. And those who tried to destroy us and our way of life will themselves be commended to the ground forever!" Once again Goetz finished with a rallying cry that was met with much cheer and admiration.

Nearly every busy hand in town was working either directly or indirectly for Goetz. Farmers harvested grain needed for the bread that the giants now expected and worked into their deal. Ranchers on the east side of the river bred cattle where the ground was more open. The bank, the mill, the hotel, saloon, all owned in one way or another by Goetz.

Goetz paid fairly, and the town prospered. Logs were coming down river at a record rate. Such was the pace that men working in different capacities at the boom site or the mill never gave heed to the men who were supposedly falling trees at the camps.

Unprecedented prosperity continued into the fall when nature took over the operation and ice began to form.

"That's ridiculous, press on. I have orders to fill, hungry mills. Push them through, ice be damned," Goetz said when told things needed to wrap for the season.

Upstream, where the water moved swiftly, the giants continued to feed the river. As ice covered the logs at the boom, work became ever more dangerous and eventually impossible. Falling in the water meant hypothermia and probable death even if a man could avoid getting sucked under the logs. Average cold made possible the snow that soon followed, which only opened the door for much more bitter cold. The sort of cold that closes your nose automatically when trying to breathe. Despite the weather, Goetz demanded they carry on operations.

Most of the giants were unbothered by the cold and continued to work as a thousand plus logs rushed down stream into the weir. They were also enjoying great prosperity. Every home had meat and bread, and logging kept them busy restoring purpose and pride.

As the logs bottled up they grew covered with snow and effectively glued themselves together with ice, locking up the river. As the pressure mounted, they jammed themselves into the river bottom with the force of a million and the speed of one. All the while the ice grew thicker.

Chapter Eight

Hard Hearts

"What do you mean the logs have stopped. I thought I made it perfectly clear that no such thing were to happen. Ice be damned I said. Why do we have giants if they can't break up a little ice?" Goetz carped.

"They say no, scared of water," Sky said.

"I thought you said she didn't speak English," Klien said.

"She only chose to not speak it I have recently discovered. My own short-comings in regards to her tongue left a bit of a communication gap. I could not take that chance. Never forget if not for her keeping her word to the giants she would kill us where we stand, as she is clearly no fan of mine," Goetz explained.

"Tell them no logs, no food," Goetz pointed his finger in Sky's chest.

"I hate to bring it up but you did say you'd carry them through the winter. Them big boys gotta eat and we certainly don't need them all riled up," Klien warned.

"Nonsense. To be fed one must work. No logs, no beef," Goetz said again.

The third night after Goetz sent the message, a collective roar of distant screams from the far end of town woke him from his abode above the bank. Big, fresh snowflakes fell in no particular hurry and there was no discernable wind.

Contrary to what one might picture, the ground did not shake when Kwah strolled through town. When an animal is built to be large, they can control their feet to the ground. That doesn't mean a few shelves of dinnerware and a handful of windows didn't rattle along his route.

People panicked and brandished weapons although they dare not fire for a couple of reasons. First of all, what if shooting him only made him angry? Nobody in town knew the temperament of a giant, but it didn't take an expert to recognize that he was not happy. Secondly, Sky Dancer sat upon his shoulders like a small child, giving direction to the home of Horace Goetz.

The aforementioned Goetz was dressed and ready on his balcony having reasonably understood quite early in the ordeal what was coming through town.

Even though Goetz was well off the ground, the two stood nearly face to face. Sky climbed down off Kwah's back and faded away into the darkness. A crowd of people trepidatiously stayed far enough away to keep escape by foot a viable option.

"Please, please everybody, come closer. May I introduce you to the giant Kwah. It has been Kwah and many like him who have been falling the lumber and sending it downriver," Goetz explained.

"What about the men? He lied. I knew something was off. Kill it," the crowd murmured collectively.

The people were shocked when they heard him speak. Many gasps were heard among them with one woman fainting dead away.

"You broke your promise. We grow hungry soon. Maybe we find other food now," Kwah said threateningly.

"Sir, good sir I can assure you I have done no such thing. Why right this very minute a rather large herd, more than enough to carry you through the winter is in route to your village. Why I only just informed your messenger Sky Dancer of this just the other day," Goetz said.

"Giants cut much wood, fill river. You must pay," Kwah said.

"Sir, like I said…," Goetz tried to speak.

"No! You lie. Sky never lie to giants," Kwah argued.

As the crowd drew nearer and more bold, a man who worked in the mill stepped forward.

"Wait a minute. You mean to tell me you been sending all our beef up river to these, these, things?" he said disgusted.

"Meanwhile we gotta pay top dollar and for what, so these freeloaders can get a hand out off all our hard work?" the man complained.

"Kwah took a long step towards the man who had no time to react. Picking him up by the waist, Kwah threw him over the bank building. His airborne screams were soon replaced with the sounds of a body breaking branches high in the darkness of the trees.

Panic was nearly instant and people fled in every direction.

"You send food now! Or we take them!" Kwah said pointing to the scattering people.

"Please Mr. Kwah calm down. I assure you the cattle are on their way. As a matter of fact they should be arriving at the farm tomorrow. You will have all you need. Furthermore, you must know that I always keep my word. I forgive you that one man, as any man should have known better, but harm one citizen of this town and I can assure you an army of men so vast as to shake the very ground with their approach will be summoned. Men with many cannons, men who will never stop coming until every last giant is no more," Goetz told him.

Aside from the closing doors in the distance, the air between the two had become so silent that the flakes could be heard stacking up on the ground.

"Maybe I just kill you now," Kwah said.

"The results would be the same, and then you could enjoy the added benefit of returning to your village with the grand news that you have doomed them all for no apparent reason," Goetz said aggressively.

Kwah pointed his extraordinarily thick finger at Goetz.

"Cows tomorrow or I will come back. We all come back," Kwah walked around the back of the bank and retrieved the body of the man from the trees before returning to speak to Goetz who was watching him through the windows.

"Him I take," Kwah said as he carried the man's limp body out of town. This time there were no screams and nobody stood out and watched. The last thing people wanted was his attention.

After the people were sure Kwah was out of town they returned to the bank building. It had been decided that Goetz had been deceitful by not telling them about the giants and he could no longer be trusted.

"For Heaven's sake what would I have told you? That giants lived three days ride up the river? How many of you would have gone to see for yourselves because you would not have believed me? I tell you now each and every one of you would have been killed," he explained.

"What about the men? The men who didn't come back with you and the sheriff?" one of the people yelled.

"Regretfully yes. It was indeed due to the giants," Goetz hung his head in shame.

"Why did he take that man? Get the army up here. Did I hear him say they'd eat us? So there weren't no Indians?" were among the furious barrage of questions.

"Why send men to die? I saw what they are capable of. Bullets simply deflect from their skin. They are fast, faster than men. Faster than deer. And they are strong, stronger than the largest bears. Why, it is nothing for them to tear a man limb from limb. You all saw what they did to Tyler Howard. They can kill ten men in the time it will take for you to soil yourself at their roar."

"Look at what we have done, what we have built. They only require to be left alone to their work, work that benefits us. My greatest regret was trusting the Indian girl for it was her who has stabbed us all in our backs. It was her who told false tales to the giants. All just to get back at me. Me, the man who single handedly slayed her captor and set her free! I take back what I said before God. She is no longer to be trusted. Find her, bring her to me!" Goetz demanded.

The people searched the town but Sky Dancer could not be found. While they searched Goetz commanded his closest commandants to round up every cow they could lay their hands on and ready them for delivery to the giants. By the next morning, a sizeable herd was corralled and ready to travel. Later that afternoon, ten men set out to drive them north.

The cowboys were on edge after they heard what happened in town. Most weren't even there but trusted the firsthand accounts. Plus the man who was thrown and then taken, presumably for a snack, was one of them.

The first arrow creased the back brim of a cowboy's hat. As he was processing what had happened, a second arrow stuck into the neck of the horse on which he rode. The horse reared back flinging him to the ground.

"Giants!" he yelled running, panicking.

Dairy cows, beef cattle, young and old all spooked together and stampeded towards the river. Waiting men dressed in furs on saddleless horses redirected them, while others continued to fire arrows at the cowboys.

The cowboys who did not run were finally given their chance to kill Native Americans but it did not go the way they planned. Already guiding a noisy herd amidst fear and anxiety, an ambush of the sort they endured was completely unexpected. They were out flanked, outnumbered, and out smarted. Watching from above, Sky Dancer asked a favor of the warriors.

"Manaaji iniji (Spare a man)," she asked.

One man, wounded, with multiple arrows in his legs cowered in fear, crawling to escape. Sky hopped off her horse and pinned him to the ground with her foot.

"You tell him, Goetz. You tell it was me, Sky Dancer. I already tell the big men you lie, cows not coming. If you hurry, you can beat them back to Goetz. They come now. Kill you all."

Sky grabbed a hold of the mane and slid back up onto the horse. Her words and shouts were indecipherable as she and her people took the meat for themselves.

Under the log at the first marker, two cowboys, Goetz and Klien kept careful count of the cattle that passed by one at a time.

"Forty two, forty three…I expected fifty. Tell me there are more head down the trail?" Goetz asked.

"I believe there are a few stragglers, Mr. Goetz. The boys should have 'em up here directly," a cowboy said.

Kwah stood by defensively with his arms folded.

"Like I said Kwah. I always keep my word. And the girl. Like I said, lies. Out of hate for me, she broke her word to you, to her people. Why even this very minute she is absconding with an entire herd. Food for your people. I so expected it that I bought these cattle myself, to prove I am worthy of your trust. Why, the worst that could have happened was you'd have even more meat. Once we heard the shooting, well unfortunately there can be no other explanation," Goetz said remorsefully. "Now maybe you'll believe me when I tell you I was only defending myself. The man drew his weapon on me. I had no choice. There's no way I could have known she was your liaison and I do apologize but clearly, her people cannot be trusted. Right now they are on their way to God knows where with that what belongs to you and yours. Thieves."

"How you know she get away?" Kwah asked.

"Let's just say I kept my best people with me. And a few of the others, well, family men. Getting home quickly would have been their priority." he said.

Kwah looked away as if disgusted.

"Now, about that ice wall," Goetz asked.

"It come down in springtime, when water warm. Ice dangerous for giants," Kwah said.

"Well, safety first you know. Very good then. We shall be in touch," Goetz said as he and his men turned and headed back to town.

"We are sure gonna need a hell of a lot more cows, Mr. Goetz," Klien said.

"Nonsense. What's the point in having giants if they won't do giant work for us? Besides, now that they know the truth, our people want revenge. I have already sent word to Snelling. A contingent will be in town directly upon our return. There will be not one more cow, nor chicken, nor loaf of bread. And then they will come, and we will be ready," Goetz said.

"And what about all them cows we took from our own people last night? The ones the girl got?" Klien asked.

"Don't worry, the Army will be sent to deal with them as well. Trust me, they hold in their chests hard hearts for Indians who steal from white settlers. I doubt a single one should survive," Goetz said. "Very doubtful indeed."

Chapter Nine

Calling All Cars…

More than twenty years passed since Sky Dancer first set eyes on the giant's village. She came upon it as most did, by way of her people from the forested hills east of the river to the place of the smoking stones. She was small and quite young, not even six years old.

She had come of age and it was her turn to learn the ropes. Sky was the youngest in a family whose sole community purpose was to be liaison to the giants. It was an honor passed down from generation to generation. Now, years later as an adult woman, she is the last of her bloodline, feared and respected by her people as the one who wields the power of the giants.

Winter came hard this far north. Smoke trickled from nearly every chimney of the giant's village hidden beneath the snow. Sky's breath was cold smoke, braving the onslaught of winter alone. Her people will not come here. They were afraid. The ground opened up before her, an immense trap door made from logs as wide as a man's waist and twice as long.

"Well?" Kwah asked.

Sky smiled and danced her horse sideways revealing a long single file line of mixed bovines walking into the village behind her. Giants came out of the ground as if they were hatching bugs, scooped them up and carried them back underground. The eight fattest were strung together and tied off to a tree.

"For your people," Kwah said.

"We thank you sir but we cannot for we must run. He has summoned his army. He will send them after my people," she said.

Kwah thought about her words for a few minutes before answering.

"Then he must come to us. It was Kwah's idea to take cows from the men. Bring people here, stay in hills along river there," Kwah said pointing to the bluffs north of his village.

"If they come, they will come here. We fight together. How long?" Kwah asked.

"Spring, if they are smart. No way they get through all this cold and snow. There's more. It was too easy. He knew," Sky warned.

"Yes, he betray. It is what his kind do. His pride make him tell me what he knows is wrong," Kwah said.

"My people will be afraid to come here. They fear the giants," she said.

"Tell them to stay in valley. Giants will not go where I say not to go. If your people come here, nobody might see them again," Kwah said.

"We'll collect them when we come back?" Sky asked motioning to the cows.

"Good, good," Kwah said nodding in agreement.

"And then I will go down and take his life. I will end this all. For everyone," she said.

"There is only one end, until then it never ends. I go call," Kwah said dipping back down inside his lair.

"Who?" Sky yelled as the door had already closed.

"Giants," came the reply from beneath the ground, if words could sound like earthquakes.

Giants, historically few and far between, adapted a communication technique not uncommon in the animal kingdom. Much like some species of whale, or elephants, giants use a form of infrasound. The extremely low frequency waves vibrate below the level of human hearing and can travel through the earth for thousands of miles.

Giants have been using infrasound to communicate for eons for a variety of reasons such as finding the opposite sex, help, or just plain loneliness. The most important call was the 'all giants'. This call must be repeated by every giant who receives it as to reach every corner of the earth. It was best started on bedrock, like a cliffside or a river bottom. This would help the first message to carry loud and clear.

There was pounding of fists coupled with low moans and 'huts'. To an outside observer it would appear as if the giant had lost its mind. 'All giant' calls were not common. For Kwah it would not only be the first he'd made, but the only one he was ever aware of outside of giant folklore. Due to resonance and time, once he hears the call return to him from five directions, he will know the message was received by all.

They trickled in, usually at night avoiding men under any circumstance. One here, one there, then it might take a couple days before any more giants found them. More than a month had passed before 'he' came to the village. But 'he' changed everything.

He was an old giant, older than Bome. And he did not come alone, the one with him, his son was also larger than Bome, a fact not lost on the other giants.

"We have come to seek the one and answer the call. I am Le Vieux, a name given to me by men for I do not recall my own. It means 'the old'. This is my son, he is Le Jeune, the young, a name also given by men."

"I am Kwah. Why do you let men name you? As pets?"

The old giant's voracious denial shook the snow from the tree tops, "Nooo!"

"I do not recall my father's name, so I can have no name. My son, the same. It was men who saved me from the ocean when I was the young one. They find me on the sand

and breathe life back into me. I fought at their sides, killing many for a very long time," Le Vieux explained.

"And your son?" Kwah asked.

"Lejeune does not know the blood. He is a friend to men," Le Vieux said.

"How does this come to pass old one? From where is it do you hail? Where was your tribe?" Kwah asked.

Le Vieux took many long moments to answer. Le Jeune sat down at his side offering him water from a carved wooden bowl.

"Men saved Le Vieux so I say men good. Help them fight bad men. After so much killing, Le Vieux not see much good. Other giants were made to fight me but Le Vieux was too strong. I say no to killing them and men grew angry. Together we left the world of men and travel long times towards the rising sun until we find another sea. We build another boat and sail small land to small land. On the other side we go towards warm air and find a forest big enough for giants."

"Two times you say men saved you. Saved you from where? What do you mean another boat?" Kwah asked.

"Le Vieux was not yet grown. I was set on one of two great ships giants built and told to watch the oxen below. I could see the other far ahead, taking up so much of where the sun goes into the water. It was the ship of my father. He kept me away to cheat the death of the ocean. Mine hit rocks below and split open. Water filled in, killing the oxen and almost Le Vieux. Father's ship fall below the waves where he took with him the name I could not recall. On this day, all was lost," Le Vieux lamented.

"I know this tale. It is the tale of a great rift between the giants. It is how we came to this world. It was your boat old one. It was not lost. It was repaired and sailed on to new lands. These are my truths you speak of, the tales of my past as well. I know who your father was, he is legend, the mighty Koros. And you are his, the son of Koros, thought lost to the sea," Kwah explained.

Le Vieux looked at Kwah as if to kill him, anger welling up in his eyes as they glossed over.

"So you know my name?" Le Vieux asked.

"I am sorry old friend. I do not. I only heard son of Koros. If this is how you should choose to be known, I welcome you son of Koros, and the son of the son of Koros!" Kwah toasted.

Le Vieux stood and placed both of his immense hands on Kwah's shoulders. His anger melting to gratification.

"You have given me much. I am as my name says and I cannot give much in return. But him, he is also as his name says, and he will give enough for two."

Le Jeune stood up tall raising his fist high in the air. He towered above the others, making most look average and others downright small. Kwah placed his closed fist against Le Jeune's chest.

"Choose your name large one. Choose and be forever feared among men," Kwah demanded.

Le Jeune recoiled and took a step back.

"What gives you pause? Your father has spoken, the name of his father is known, so yours can now be known. Choose," Kwah told him again.

"I do not want men to fear me. Killing is why we are here. Men will always try to kill what they fear. I will not choose. My name will be known how I will be known, the one who lets men live," Le Jeune said.

"These men are bad, they kill their own. They kill our ox. They try to kill us. They lie. They take. They destroy. Many men come to help them, to bring big guns to kill giants." Kwah explained.

Le Jeune's face curled as he heard more details about the men he was called to fight. After some time he gave Kwah his answer.

"Then we kill only the bad ones, make more room for the good ones." Together the giants in unison as a sort of rallying cry, let out a bloodcurdling howl so loud it was said that it would carry on forever. Legend tells of snow being knocked off the trees for a hundred miles in every direction.

In Stillwater people thought it was the wind and to this day when they hear it, many still do.

Chapter Ten

The Bad Ones

"My people have made camp. It warms quickly. The snow will leave us soon. I will go now and kill the one," Sky Dancer told Kwah.

Sky intended on entering town under the cover of darkness but it was the darkness that gave her fair warning. Dozens of illuminated tents pitched in perfect rows in the fields above town glowed like Christmas lights. In the higher fields most of the snow had already melted away leaving muddy roads lined with cannons on wheels made for wagons. Sky returned to the village at best speed.

"And so it has begun," Kwah said after hearing the news.

"Tell your people to burn the tents in the night. Cause many screams. Destroy many big guns. Leave a trail on town side of the river to follow. Cross where shallow before waters rise too high where big guns cannot cross. Bring them to us. Take people towards the sun out of danger. Leave a few," Kwah instructed.

In the middle of the next night Sky and her people did as requested. Men with arrows lit ablaze rained fire onto the canvas tents. Soldiers scrambled through the smoke and flames searching for snow to put out the fires.

Another group rushed through on horseback, using ropes to tip and drag the cannons out of camp. The cannons were heavier than anticipated and the element of surprise quickly evaporated. Of the eight men on horseback, six were killed and most of the big guns remained unaffected.

Still more of Sky's people ran through town, tipping wagons, breaking what they could and shooting in the air. They were mindful to move quickly and not hurt anyone without cause or in case of self-preservation. Just as quickly as they arrived, they rode out of town.

These actions followed an edict handed down by Kwah who was convinced to show mercy by Le Jeune who believed most people were good.

Chaos erupted across the town as Goetz's men readied themselves as a secondary force behind the soldiers. Taking full advantage of the confusion Sky worked her way into town playing the part of a cowboy in an obvious hurry. Nobody looked twice.

Goetz watched the attack unfold from his upstairs rear window, half-dressed sipping tea from a dainty cup. He never expected a black powder device to be set off on the opposite side balcony overlooking the street. Given the circumstances, either few noticed, or they were more concerned with the war that just spawned in their once quiet frontier town.

Sky, standing on her saddle jumped to the balcony and was standing over Goetz inside before he had a chance to figure out what happened. Uncharacteristically without speaking a word Goetz scrambled for his pistol tucked in its holster. It was laying on the floor close by after previously hanging on a coat rack disrupted during the explosion. Sky clubbed him unconscious before he could reach it and then hit him again just for good measure. She dropped him over the balcony tied by his waist dangling him over the street below.

Once on her horse she cut the rope and fashioned him to the saddle before riding off into the darkness.

The next morning at first light the army reassembled and made ready to pursue the native tribe. Goetz's men, led by sheriff Klien were unable to find a body or any other sign of his demise. Choosing to be paid over getting killed, they chose to search for him although their fate and the army's seemed hopelessly intertwined.

Besides superficial wounds, no soldiers were killed during the attack, which emboldened them further. The commander believed the story of giants was nothing more than a hoax, a clever trick of the Indians meant to scare settlers away.

"I saw no giants. Did anyone see a giant last night?" the colonel laughed and mocked.

"It was just as I had suspected. Savages. Which savages I cannot say with any certainty but rest assured, we will know soon enough," he added.

By noon that day the army, two hundred strong with eight cannons marched North up the west side of the St. Croix

River following the trail laid out by Sky's warriors. On the first day they didn't even make it half way to the river crossing.

Progress was slow. The trails were thin and muddy from the quickly melting snow and the forest on either side was too steep to transverse. After most of another day in the saddle, they found the oddities, the first marker and the oversized deadfall trap. The colonel had also recognized its design as being of Paiute decent as he was no stranger to killing Native Americans. To him, it was just further proof that they were dealing with Indians and he used his theory to motivate the men.

By the evening of the second day they reached the river crossing that looked more like suicide than a way across.

"Yes sir, we took it for miles. Upstream it just gets bigger and wider. This is it," the scout reported to the colonel.

"Tonight we will make camp before fording the river in the morning. They clearly crossed here and so therefore must we," the colonel commanded.

As Kwah predicted, the river was too high and swift for cannons or wagons to cross. The ones that tried were taken away by the current. Only men clinging to horses were able to make their way across in water that was normally ankle deep.

Downstream at the boom site, the river was backing up. Huge chunks of ice previously married to the shore clunked into a jagged pile interwoven with logs that waited all winter for their chance to float again. As the water rose, the damn widened, drowning the canyon behind it, turning it into an icy, churning lake.

Without the advice of his scouts who did not return, the colonel drove his army up the steep trail and straight into the heart of the giant village to the place of the smoking stones. Only sparse patches of snow remained here. In the distance, six native men on horseback acting on orders from Kwah, launched arrows towards the colonel and his army. An all out charge ensued.

It wasn't until nearly all of them were up to speed when the ground very unexpectedly opened up before them.

At least half of the men immediately faceplanted, horses and all directly into open holes. Their momentum caused them to be unable to stop. Others dove free of the horses only to fall into adjacent holes that moments prior did not exist. It seems the giants could only open so many doors at once. Men who managed to gain their footing were quickly brushed in like so much rubbish.

Of those who were on the back sides of the doors when they flung open, their fates were not as well-spoken of. Many were injured and in some cases, killed. The giants moved quickly shutting the doors and securing them with freshly installed bolts across the tops, much too large for a dozen men to move. Some hatches were secured with dead horses and others with large stones.

Within minutes the entire division was captured without firing a shot and only a handful of men accidentally killed. The men were heard to be unhappy, but trapped, nevertheless.

"All hear me now," Kwah said to his giants. We must go from this place. Many will come. Will never stop until all giants gone. You go your way, you go your way," he said pointing at the crowd. This is how we will survive."

"Not so fast!" Sky yelled soaking wet in the saddle, her prisoner precariously absent.

"The bad ones, remember? They are coming," she said.

Chapter Eleven

Remember him?

A low laugh, quiet at first but building to a crescendo of thunder rocked the crowd of giants. At least one of them was suddenly quite happy.

"We kill bad ones," laughed the mighty giant Bome, cannons at the ready.

The giants were not looking forward to crossing the river. Even with their immense weight and strength, it meant more surface area for the water to push against.

Kwah watched from shore as they advanced. The largest cyclops stood up with such a surprised look on his face that one might have felt sorry for him. At least as sorry as one could feel for a man eater as the cannonball easily ripped through his eyeball and out the back of his head. Nobody saw where the cannonball went. The cyclops went down like a tree, his body sucked away by the river.

The second cannonball was ironically caught by the smallest of the giants, the cave dweller who would make tools. He disappeared under the water so quickly as the extent of the damage was undefinable and he never rose again.

Seven of the cannons the army brought to the party were fired from the opposite shoreline in unison by the much smaller posse of men who were searching for Goetz. One of the cannons did not fire. Three missed anything altogether but the last one left a crease in Kwah's forehead dropping him straight onto his giant butt. Although it didn't puncture his thick skin, it left an impression deep enough to comfortably cradle a banana.

The giants turned back as men reloaded the cannons. Men fired rifles that did not kill the giants but stung badly enough that it got old extremely quickly.

Once regrouped, with their leader concussed and confused many of the giants decided to take Kwah's original advice and set out on their own. Especially after seeing what the cannons could do to them.

"I fight," Bome said. "Who fight with Bome?"

Of the giants who volunteered, most were very old and knew they could never get by in the world of men. Some who had been there, swore they would never go back. Only one young giant joined the group, the son of the son of Koros, Le Jeune.

"I fight to make sure it ends," he said.

Sky watched from the valley's highest point as the giants dispersed up and down the river. Goetz, helplessly gagged and bound to a tree next to her could only wonder what she had instore for him.

"You two come with Bome. You load," Bome said to two other giants.

From the opposite side, high up the rocky bank, Bome opened fire on the cannons below. Having run out of cannonballs years ago, he loaded his cannons with stones resulting in defacto shotguns that devastated human flesh. The dozen or so men manning the cannons were cut to ribbons in short order.

Now the accidental general, Bome took a small contingent south to the boom site while he sent others to pursue the men.

"What is this boom site? Why do we go there?" Le Jeune asked.

"Another place to cross. We can cut them off," Bome said.

The giants found this agreeable and moved at best speed which compared to a man was considerable.

They passed the great fields, home to the last of the Vibrant Oxen before descending to the valley of the boom. A valley which was very much full of water. Le Jeune, lagging behind, taking in the scenery noticed the ox in the distance were standing in an odd configuration. When he came upon them, he couldn't decide whether to be appalled or impressed. He chose impressed.

Sky Dancer rode the neck of the fourth ox, whispering sweetly into its ear as it backed up towards three others who were already standing rump to rump. Tied to each of the three ox's tails was a short section of rope tied in turn onto each limb of Horace Goetz.

"If you wish to make this man suffer. I might have a better idea," Le Jeune told her.

"I wish to pull him apart, slowly," she said.

***

Bome's team made it to the flat ice sheet under the dam. The ice below them was still quite thick as water rushed out in small rivers below the dam. In the distance but quickly approaching they could hear much gunfire as the other giants pushed the remaining men south.

Some of the pursuing giants broke off after taking too many bullets. One was killed early on by a booby trap made from a swinging log sharpened to a point. The pierced his stomach and left him to bleed out. Another giant fell down the cliffside out of sight leaving his condition unknown but based on the moaning he was assumed out for the duration.

The remaining few managed to greatly reduce the number of men in Goetz's employ with simple stones, clubs and extra-large axes. The archaic warfare proved effective considering the simple stones weighed as much as a horse, which giants were also fond of throwing at men.

Bome made ready his cannons and waited until he could see them coming along the cliffside trail across the river. There were glimpses of men, but nothing worthy of fire. Unbeknownst to Bome, no amount of money was deemed worthy by the surviving members of the posse and those who lived only wished to escape. It was the only reason they set one last trap.

"Ha! Men," Bome said joyfully raising the cannon to his shoulder like a man would fire a rifle.

Across the river, high up on the bluff two of the fastest men ran the cliffside trail. Bome could not get the shot off, hesitating when he noticed three giants closing on them quickly. At the opportune moment, just as the men crossed the trigger point, five large logs poured off the top of the boulders above the trail, rolling horizontally. Two giants were pushed over the side while the last one stepped poorly and spun his ankle before also joining his friends a hundred feet below.

"No!" Bome yelled infuriated. "Bome kill them all!"

His voice carried a great distance, far enough for even Le Jeune to hear.

"We had better hurry," he said.

Bome fired his cannons one after another into the dam. Huge cracks tore open and water rushed through. In moments, he was unable to hold his place on the ice against the rushing water. Le Juene and Sky arrived at the very moment Bome and his accompanying team were swept into the deep water and lost forever.

The damn was irreparably damaged and as much water flowed through the breach, it was a pittance compared to what was still stored behind it, ready to burst at any moment. Downstream, the town of Stillwater quickly began to flood.

People who were able took to higher ground. The tallest structure nearer the water was the first Lutheran church. Its wooden steeple was rapidly filling with the freshly anointed homeless congregation. The pastor looked out the belltower like the captain of a ship destined to flounder. Goetz had been missing since the start of the melee and people now looked to the pastor for leadership.

When the dam broke, a wall of water, ice and logs a hundred feet high and a thousand feet wide came barreling down the river valley dozing everything in its path alive, dead, or otherwise. It rolled with the sound of a summer's worth of thunder and tornadoes and shook the very ground to the point that even those with four legs could no longer stand.

From the steeple they could see it coming. Birds flocking out in front of it flying for their lives. Some of the people froze in fear, others because they were awestruck. Klien, who strangely decided not to pursue the giants and stay in town, wondered where Goetz had gone. The pastor, for lack of having the ability to reason, wandered from his prayers ever so slightly. At least long enough to answer Klien's question.

"I'd say that's him right over there," the pastor said pointing his trembling finger.

He was fixated on a new storm approaching, with new thunder and new fear. Unlike the rushing water and ice, this one had a beat. It played a song all too familiar to the farmers, the rhythmic beat of pounding hooves.

Not one, not two or even three, but five great oxen, shoulder to shoulder harnessed by the anchor chains of river boats plowed through the flooded town, pushing aside or demolishing everything in their path. Standing tall on the back of the largest and most Vibrant Ox of them all, Le Jeune drove the team fearlessly forward, Sky Dancer at his side. Between the horns of that ox, dead center, tied tightly, ungagged and stripped to his undergarments, Horace Goetz watched his fate unfold before him like a bug stuck to the front license plate of a crashing car.

The church stood on the waterfront, part of a long line of buildings including two hotels, a restaurant, a saloon, a school and a myriad of retail stores.

In unison, horns locked, the team lowered their heads and dislodged all of the buildings at once. With the entire block clamped in the horns of the oxen, Le Jeune pushed them forward like a giant plow, across the cracking ice until they were face to face with the icy deluge.

They say it was only a moment before the collision when it happened. One of those snapshots in time when the minutes on a clock were merely a suggestion. It might have only been a few seconds but it was a scene forever trapped in metaphoric amber.

The pastor became enamored with the bravery of the giant who he fully expected to kill them all. Now this giant was clearly risking his own life to save the people. It was at this moment he recalled a biblical reference of which he was particularly fond.

"Is not this he that destroyed them which called on his name in Jerusalem?" the pastor preached loudly.

"I shall call him Paul!" he said referring to giant.

Paul was one of the twelve apostles of Christ, an ex-Pharisee who spent his youth persecuting the very Christians he would eventually follow into biblical infamy.

"Let's do it babe!" Paul yelled as he crashed the buildings into the wave.

The sky cracked lightning and thunder from the tremendous impact. Clouds parted ways and a cold wind blasted so far down river some say it caused it to snow in the gulf. Goetz disintegrated and before she lost her grip, Sky was able to enjoy the sweet taste of revenge. Neither was ever seen again. Only the giant had the strength to hold on. The land on the east side broke down and liquified like quicksand and the river cut a new course, sparing whoever and whatever was left of the town.

"Kwah retired to the forests, went north the last I heard. Could tell by the look in his eye I was never gonna see him again. And Le Jeune? I guess the name took cause everybody knew him as Paul from then on. Sadly only one of the great Vibrant Oxen survived the day, the big blue one. Yessir from that day those two become the bestest of friends. I heard they went north to Minnesota country somewhere. Kept the old logging tradition alive I guess," the Old Man said.

THE KICK-ASS END

ABOUT THE AUTHOR

Daniel Rehm became a full-time writer after a long career in the paint and industrial coatings industry. He still has nightmares about it.

Dan wrote *The Giant Lumbermen of Stillwater* in February 2025 in celebration of the first Literary Libations event at Lift Brewery in Stillwater, MN. The story feeds our imaginations about giants in the land of Minnesota along the St. Croix River Valley during the time of Stillwater's early settlers.

The year prior, Dan wrote *Knife Lake Nightmare: Dorothy Vs. Darlene*, in celebration of the Harvest Moon Festival in Ely, MN. The story imagines the meeting between Dorothy, of Knife Lake, and Darlene Hatchka, her antithesis and a character that appears in many of Dan's works as an evil, carnivorous, witch.

Dan's work includes *Let Flowers Be Flowers*, written between 2008 and 2011, which includes various landscapes he knows very well – from the coulee area of western Wisconsin to the boreal forest of the Boundary Waters Canoe Area, and brings to life the various relationships among men and their families in addition to the exploration of the sociopathic nature of a killer – what motivates a killer, what haunts a killer, and what purpose that killer believes he has in his life. *Flowers* is where the character Darlene Hatchka first appears, as one of the BWCA holdouts when the area was first preserved.

In 2020, Dan wrote the series *The Adventures of Philippine Maximine, PI* in an effort to capture the essence of some of the characters found in *Flowers*. Philippine Maxine returns in the 2022 book titled *The Troll Hunters*, where Dan weaves some of the fun of *Philippine Maximine, PI* into the dark undertones of *Flowers*. He was excited to introduce new characters as well as refresh readers with some old and dear friends in this modern and timely standalone thriller.

Dan launched Rudbeckia Productions, LLC in 2020 to publish his work and vowed to never sell another gallon of paint as long as he lived.

Dan can be reached at contact@DanRehm.com.

Rudbeckia
PRODUCTIONS